NO ESCAPE

NOEL COUGHLAN

CONTENTS

NO ESCAPE

Cover by Ivan Cakic

Edited by Proofed to Perfection (http://www.proofedtoperfection.com/)

Published by Photocosmological Press (http://photocosm.org/)

Paperback Edition: ISBN:978-1-910206-19-5

NO ESCAPE

Crouched behind a clump of rusty bushes, Tharo stroked his sunken cheeks. Remembering the lies tattooed in white on his green-black skin—*honor* on the left cheek, *truth* on the right—he dropped his hand. In the evening light, beneath two marbled moons, red Ruis and white Neor, a traveler and his mule trod across the blushing dunes toward him. Tharo primed his crossbow with his last bolt and waited for them to draw closer.

The weapon would serve to deter his victim from a fight he could not possibly win. Tharo needed the mule, but he had no desire to kill for it. In the distant highlands, his tattoos—the marks of an elite Warserk of the Kaplar Empire—would have cowed all but the most foolhardy into submission, but here in this foreign land, the crossbow proved to be a better threat.

He winced as a hot, dusty breeze tickled his face and flapped the empty sling against his battered breastplate. *Please, gods, halt this infernal wind before it wakes the princess!* An eerie stillness immediately settled over the desert. A coincidence—that was all. Tharo's gods had abandoned him long ago.

"Eh eh eh."

He looked down at the little, green-black face peeping out of the dusty, red bundle of swaddling. The blue-green jadeite tear on her forehead gleamed in the evening light. "Shush, Drinith."

The baby whimpered. Any moment now, she would bawl.

Holding the crossbow in one hand, Tharo waved at her. "Shush, please." They needed the mule to evade the souldiviner hunting them, to drag out the pursuit a little longer. Sooner or later, their stalker and his henchmen would find them. Souldiviners always caught their prey.

Drinith's piercing wail reminded Tharo of her soother in his backpack. He bit his lip as he popped the dummy in her mouth. Mercifully, she took it. As she made contented sucking sounds, he eyed the lone traveler. The man continued at the same plodding pace toward them, apparently oblivious to her cry. He must be deaf or at least hard of hearing.

Tharo released a shaky breath and wiped his slick forehead with the back of his hand. Why hadn't he thought of the soother earlier? He had never spent much time around children. As a Warserk, he had forsworn family. As much as he had come to dote on Drinith, he hated being her guardian. He had never known fear before his emperor entrusted his daughter to him.

The traveler's dark skin had the blue tinge typical of lowlanders. Even in his loose garb, he must swelter in this heat. The fuzzy, white beard extending from his jawline coiled like a scroll. As he drew closer, Tharo could hear him mumbling grumpily to himself or perhaps the mule.

Tharo tensed to pounce. He glanced again at Drinith. Suppose some predator lurking in the bushes attacked her while he dealt with the old man. No, it was best not to think of it. He couldn't bring her with him. She mustn't be implicated in this crime. It must be his shame alone. Taking a deep breath, he rose and plunged through the brush.

The old man halted. The curiosity in his stare quickly turned to anger. "Bandit!" he yelled, waving a fist.

"I want your beast," Tharo said clearly and loudly, aiming the crossbow at him. "You can keep your goods."

"That's kind of you," the ancient muttered. "And how am I supposed to carry them to my village? By the time I get help from there, they'll be gone."

Was Drinith crying again? Tharo glanced back at the bushes.

The old man's head nodded angrily. "I can tell by the green cast of your skin you're a highlander. Nothing good ever comes from there—only thieving vagabonds." His face creased with disgust. He spat his anger on the ground. "That's what I think of highlanders. That's what I think of robbers."

"Not every highlander is a criminal," Tharo said.

The old man snorted. "Says a thief."

The undeniable truth of his insult stung. However, Tharo couldn't let the old fool have the last word. "You had better hope I don't add murder to my crimes."

The old man's blue eyes widened. "Take what you will and leave me in peace."

Holding the crossbow in one hand, Tharo drew his knife and approached the mule. The crossbow wobbled up and down as he cut the cord holding its cargo on its back, but at this range, it couldn't miss its target. With a snap of the cord, the bags spilled onto the sand.

Tharo slit his thumb against the edge of his knife before sheathing it. A Warserk's knife must always taste blood once drawn.

As he reached to free the reins from the old man's grip, Tharo's head tingled. *No, not now!* The prickle expanded into a gnawing buzz as though a thousand flies filled his brain. The souldiviner again attempted to locate him. The pain forced Tharo's eyes shut. "Leave me be!"

As the old man wrenched the crossbow from Tharo's trembling hands, Tharo pulled the trigger. A punch to Tharo's jaw sent him reeling backwards. The *whack* of the ground against the back of Tharo's head severed the souldiviner's connection. The silhouette of the crossbow rose like a scythe above him, then plummeted. As he rolled clear, it crunched against the ground.

The lowlander fell upon him. Tharo's struggle to suppress the reflex to kill paralyzed him momentarily under the onslaught of his fists. A single well-aimed punch knocked the old man senseless. Tharo shoved him off and scrambled to his feet. His attacker lay sprawled on the ground, groaning.

"Stupid fool," Tharo said. "You could have gotten yourself killed." Blood smeared his hand as he rubbed the sting from his lower lip. He was the greater fool to hesitate when attacked. The old man could have killed him if he had been a better fighter. Tharo shook his head. Where were the combat instincts he had honed from the age of seven? Guilt had caused him to falter. He had always lived by his honor, but now it had become his enemy.

He picked up his crossbow. The string had snapped, but worse, the stock had cracked, rendering the weapon useless. In frustration, he flung it away. He grabbed the mule by its reins and led it over to Drinith. Scooping her off the ground, he nestled her into her sling.

He led the mule back to the old man and peered down at him. The lowlander winced as he sat up. Tharo shied from his contemptuous stare. Someday he would return here and make amends. Someday.

"What's your name?" Tharo asked.

"Hetcham," the old man said. The strain in his voice made Tharo examine him more closely. Blood covered the hand he pressed to his side. The crossbow bolt protruded between his fingers.

No. "I never meant to harm you," Tharo pleaded.

Hetcham flopped back down onto the ground. Cradling Drinith, Tharo knelt beside his victim and checked for respiration. No breath tickled Tharo's cheek as he placed it against the old man's mouth. Hetcham was dead.

"Damn you!" Tharo yelled, waving his fist at the sky, but his curse was not directed against the gods but their greatest servant. If the Oracle of Godsdoor had taken in the princess, Tharo wouldn't have had to travel through this inhospitable desert, robbing and murdering old men. Terrified that the heathen invaders would raze his temple, the Oracle had refused Drinith sanctuary. By turning his back on the sole surviving heir of the Kaplar crown, he had damned more than Drinith. He had doomed his people to hopeless slavery under their new Javlohm overlords.

As much as Tharo regretted Hetcham's death, he couldn't dally over a corpse. Hopefully some of the old man's people would soon stumble across his body. Tharo climbed onto the mule and dug his heels into its sides. Its whinny contorted into a squeaky bray as it set off at a trot. The princess bawled, doubtless frightened by the commotion. It took time for Tharo to calm her again.

A yearning for his beloved mountains made him glance back in their direction, but they had long sunk beneath the flat horizon. How far did this desert stretch? What lay beyond it? The Oracle had said to head east, but his advice could have been merely a ploy to rid himself of Drinith. Tharo should have talked to Hetcham. Information would have been more valuable than the mule. With nothing better to steer him, he had no choice but to follow the Oracle's direction.

Tharo traveled through the shivery night while Drinith slept in her sling. In competing moonlights, the mule and its new owner cast shadows in two directions as they trod across dunes. Tharo needed to find water or a place to shelter from the sun before it climbed into the sky. And he needed sleep.

Not even the chill could relieve his exhaustion. His leaden eyelids drifted shut only for him to startle awake as he shifted sideways on the mule's back. He could have fallen off and injured Drinith—or worse. The burning memory of his shameful surrender to fatigue kept him alert thereafter.

The first dab of blue touched the eastern horizon when the mule slowed to a stop. Tharo's insistent kicks failed to budge it. Perhaps it needed a rest. Cradling Drinith with one arm, he carefully dismounted. As he gently rested her on the sand to relieve his aching shoulder, the mule yanked the reins from his hand.

"Come back!" he cried, racing after it, but the fleeing mule's whinny mocked him. Drinith's soaring wail halted his pursuit. He couldn't abandon Drinith to chase after the animal. As he ran back to her and lifted her up, the mule disappeared behind the dunes. Hetcham had died for nothing.

———

Tharo wiped his forehead with the back of his hand. In this intense afternoon heat, he should have dripped sweat, but his skin was as dry as the surrounding desert. Two days had passed since Hetcham's murder, and Tharo's plight had only worsened. He had no food. Not even a drop of water remained to rattle in his metal canteen. The rolling dunes and desiccated scrub had long ago given way to an unending flatness. And the sun beat down on him, a weight in itself, pressing him to fall upon the scalding sands and die. Only Drinith's presence gave him the strength to resist. She kept him fighting for each step across this hopeless waste.

He glanced at the wobbly line of footprints behind him. No point worrying about the souldiviner stumbling across their trail. They must keep moving. The impossible might happen—they might yet escape their pursuer. Hadn't that old fortune-teller promised Tharo years ago he'd die laughing? A charlatan, of course, living off the curious and the naive. Peddlers didn't possess such powers. They were the preserve of men and women learned in the mystical arts, like souldiviners and the Oracle.

No! The Oracle was a worse fraud than any fortune-teller. Tharo's fists tensed as he remembered his smug face, swollen like a leech on the benefactions of his gullible followers. Damn him. He should have taken Drinith in. She'd be safe now instead of slowly cooking to death in this pitiless wasteland.

Beneath the shade of his cloak, she began to whimper. Shushing, he gently rocked her back and forth. She would be dead but for the Oracle's miraculous gift—a nursing bottle that never ran out of milk. Tharo should have been thankful to the coward for that crumb of generosity, but resentment bit too deep.

A painful whir filled his head, setting his whole body aquiver. The souldiviner returned to crawl inside his skull, looking through his eyes, hearing with his ears, sniffing through his nostrils, tasting the dryness of his mouth, feeling the burn of the desert against his skin.

Tharo forced a grin. *Feel my smile. I don't know where I am so you'll learn nothing by poking around inside my head.* He stared down at Drinith. *Look. The princess still lives. I'll make sure she gets across this desert. I'll keep her safe until she is old enough to hunt down your master and restore all you took from us.*

The buzz waned. The hollowness of Tharo's threat as he brandished a crying baby must have amused the souldiviner.

Drinith had to be thirsty. Tharo removed the little bottle from his pocket. He rubbed off the stray sand grains clinging to the nipple and offered the milk to her. Her contented feeding made him lick his blistered lips. His mouth was so parched. No, however tempting it might be to sip from her bottle, he couldn't risk spoiling whatever magical charm made it work.

She turned away from the bottle, having had enough. He rested her against his shoulder and rubbed her back until she burped. As he slipped her back into her sling, his eyes drifted to the bottle. She couldn't survive out here for long without him. A sip couldn't hurt, could it? He lifted the bottle to his mouth and, closing his lips around the nipple, tried to draw a few drops of moisture from it. His heart sank as no sound came from the bottle, no drop of sustaining milk splashed his parched mouth. He probed with his tongue for the slightest trace of dampness.

Nothing. Whatever spell caused the milk flow didn't work for him.

Panic gripped him. His meddling might have undone the Oracle's magic.

He examined the nipple for any obvious sign of damage. His stomach twisted at the evidence of his defilement—a bead of blood clung to it. He rubbed it away with a cloth.

His hand trembled as he pressed the bottle again to Drinith's lips. She turned her head away. He persisted, eventually managing to insert the nipple in her bawling mouth. But she refused to feed from it. Sighing, he removed the bottle and drew his cloak over her again. He'd have to wait until she became hungry to learn if the bottle still worked for her. The tension of this appalling uncertainty spurred him across the desert.

A black rock rose above the shimmering horizon. Clinging to Drinith, Tharo jogged toward it as fast as he dared. It might signal the end of the desert, or at least provide respite from its heat. As he drew closer, the rock took on the shape of a prow. He sighed heavily. It must be an illusion. There could be no ship out here. But the vision persisted, growing bigger as he neared it.

Droning pain bored into his skull—*resist*. He bowed his head and squeezed his eyes shut. The souldiviner mustn't see the rock. Its distinctive shape would surely give away Tharo's location. His whole body shook as the souldiviner wriggled about beneath his skin. Tharo's eyelids fluttered as his attacker willed him to open them. He must have guessed from Tharo's determination to keep them shut that some useful clue lay nearby. Crushing pain gripped Tharo's whole body. A single souldiviner couldn't afflict this agony. There must be at least two. That would explain why the attacks had occurred so frequently.

Tharo dropped to his knees. Drinith screamed as her sling swung back and forth, knocking her repeatedly against Tharo's breastplate. With tremulous arms, he lifted her sling away from his armor. Had the souldiviners deliberately tried to injure her? They might be able to invade his senses, but they couldn't make him do anything, however much the inflicted pain insisted otherwise. And they couldn't keep this exhausting effort up forever.

A moment later, the drone eased. Afraid its abatement might be some sort of ruse, he forced himself to wait for it to disappear entirely before opening his eyes. Drinith continued to weep as he removed her from the sling and unwrapped her swaddling. Thank the gods, she showed no signs of injury. If anything happened to her... He drove the thought away with a shake of his head as he rocked her gently in his arms. "No need to be frightened, Drinith. We're safe." *Until I die of thirst, or the souldiviners catch us.*

Her father, the Emperor of Kaplar, had made it easy for them to pick up Tharo's trail. In his crown, he kept phials of his guards' blood to guarantee their loyalty, an insulting practice made sufferable only by its antiquity. By letting the Javlohm invaders take the crown intact, he not only made it easier for souldiviners to hunt down his most loyal servants, but also provided them with a means of inflicting pain across great distances.

When Drinith finally calmed, Tharo wrapped her in the swaddling again and returned her to the sling.

"Eh eh eh."

Could she be thirsty again so soon? Tharo gently pushed the bottle into her mouth. He leaned close and listened. Her sucking sounds suggested she was ingesting something. Upon removing the bottle, milk spilled from her mouth as she sought the nipple again. Thank the gods! The bottle's magic must only work for her.

His gaze followed a drop trickling down her cheek. His hand caught it as it fell. Desperation inspired him to lick his palm, but it had already dried. They must escape this heat. As soon as she was sated, he headed again for the rock. He might find shade there, or perhaps a pool of water. As he ambled closer, he spotted gray nets staked around it like spiderwebs. What use could they possibly have in this desert? Squat stone structures peeped above the edge the rock's summit—huts of some kind.

Tharo slowed. Perhaps this place had been abandoned long ago and the arid climate had preserved these relics of its previous habitation. If people still dwelt here, and if they were friendly, he might find help. On the other hand, they might prove to be as inhospitable as their desert home. Slipping his knife from its scabbard, he hid it under Drinith's sling.

The rock was indeed shaped like an enormous boat, its sides curving gently inward. Tharo rubbed one hand against the smooth, black stone. He struggled to recognize his reflection on the polished surface. Caked dirt hid his tattoos, transforming him into an anonymous highlander.

He strolled along the shaded side. It provided a welcome relief from the sun but little protection from the sweltering heat.

A head rose above the edge of the summit. A curly, black beard peeped from the shadow of a broad sun hat. "Hello! You're a long way from civilization here." The man sounded friendly enough.

"I am attempting to cross the desert," Tharo explained. "I lost my mule." His chest constricted at the lie.

"Animals have a habit of dying out here," the man

warned. "My name is Mergal. Welcome to the village of Township. Are you alone?" A dangerous question.

"Only me and this baby," Tharo said, drawing back his cloak to reveal Drinith. "Where is everyone else?"

Mergal removed his hat, revealing typical lowland features, and brushed a hand through his bushy black hair. "They've gone fishing." He yawned. "They'll be back when the sea comes in."

The man was obviously mad, but could he be dangerous?

"I'm looking for water. And a fresh mount if you have one."

"I'm sorry," Mergal said. "I'm afraid I have no beast to offer."

"Have you water?" Tharo asked. Spying what appeared to be a pool at the base of the rock, he dashed toward it.

"Don't drink that!" Mergal cried. "Seawater."

Tharo knelt and, stabbing his knife into the sand, cupped some of the filthy water in his hands and sipped. Its briny taste forced him to spit it out.

"You want water?" Mergal asked as though he only heard Tharo now.

Tharo winced. "Yes."

"Come on up and get it." A net unfurled down the side of the rock. "This is as good a ladder as any."

"I'd rather not, if you don't mind," Tharo said. "Anything might be waiting for me up there."

Mergal chuckled. "Fair point. You're a stranger, after all. Why should you trust me? I'll send down a bucket."

Tharo nicked his arm with his knife and sheathed it. How many more times must he satisfy the ghost of his honor with his own blood?

He rose wearily to his feet. The bucket spun dangerously as it descended on a rope. As soon as it was within his reach, he tugged it down so that he could peek inside. He scooped up a handful of the water within. It felt so cold sloshing in his palm.

Mergal emitted a soft chuckle. "Of course, you don't know if it's poisoned."

Tharo froze.

"Sorry," Mergal said with a sly grin. "Go ahead."

Tharo grimaced. If Mergal aimed to poison him, he would hardly be so blatant as to admit it, so Tharo slurped down the water. It tasted so sweet. A cold pulse descended his chest. His chapped lips felt rough against his fingers as he licked them to absorb every trace of moisture.

Perhaps he should wait to see if anything happened to him, but his thirst overwhelmed his caution. In this heat, the water in the bucket would evaporate quickly. Laying Drinith in the rock's fringe of shade, he knelt down, squeezed his head and hands inside the bucket, and lifted handful after handful to his mouth.

His empty canteen! In his haste to quench his thirst, he had forgotten it. He submerged it in the water. It bubbled as it filled. Stoppering it, he shook the excess water clinging to its surface back into the bucket, then scooped up the remaining pool and slurped it down. Not even the last tantalizing drop, too small for him to pick up, went to waste. He lifted the bucket and tilted it slowly until it finally trickled into his mouth. He licked up the residual moisture clinging to his hands, afraid to squander it. It might be a long time before he had another chance to quench his thirst so thoroughly again.

Drinith's bawl spurred Tharo to pick her up. Hopefully she just wanted attention. In the gently rocking cradle of his arms, her cries turned to contented gurgles. His lips hurt as he mirrored her satisfied smile.

Mergal coughed. "Are you all right down there?"

"Yes," Tharo said. "Thank you."

"You're welcome. Would you like to come up now?"

Again, the offer. "No, thank you," Tharo said. "I don't want to intrude."

"Look, the sea comes tonight with the third moon's rising. If you change your mind, I'll leave the net down. You seem like a nice man, if a bit mad being out here with your *child*."

The way he stressed the word made Tharo uncomfortable. Even if he could trust Mergal, this rock was likely to be a well-known landmark in this monotonous desert. If the souldiviners got a glimpse of it, they'd find it quickly.

Mention of the glass moon, Bawror, was an ill-omen. In the highlands, its coming brought earthquakes. Whenever it passed in front of the sun, it started great conflagrations. But what could Bawror possibly have to do with the sea? Mergal must be mad. Or he might have a more sinister motive in delaying Tharo's departure. The souldiviners might already be on their way to Township.

"We'll head on," Tharo said, returning Drinith to her sling. "Can you spare some food?"

Mergal shook his head. "If you stay for the night, I'll happily feed you, but if you intend to leave...well, that's different. It would be a waste of food. Sorry."

Again, the insistence on staying. "Thanks again for the water. And good luck with your fishing."

Mergal shook his head. "Uh uh. Don't be a fool. You're several days from anywhere, and the sea arrives this evening." He dismissed Tharo with a wave. "Your life is your own business. I can't stop you. Watch out for the silver line."

As Tharo stalked alongside Township, Mergal followed above. Tharo paused at the end of the rock, the end of its relief from the sun. However tempting, it was too dangerous to linger. Covering Drinith with his cloak, he marched on.

The buzz returned. He squeezed his eyes shut. The souldiviners mustn't learn about Township. The attack, weaker than before, passed quickly. The souldiviners must be tired. Tharo grinned at this minor victory.

"Are you all right?" Mergal called.

"I'm fine," Tharo grunted, walking on.

With every peek over his shoulder, the rock shrank. It gradually sank back into the desert. Mergal might have been mad, but his generosity had saved them. If what he said was true... Township could have been a trap and the water and the offer of food might have been bait. But supposing Tharo was indeed days from anywhere—he couldn't survive on this little canteen. He paused and gazed back again. Township had nearly disappeared. Perhaps Tharo should turn around. No. Shaking his head, he marched on.

Below Ruis and Neor, Bawror's transparent shell glinted as it peeped above the desert. Gleaming silver fringed the horizon. Some dreadful intuition warned Tharo that this was the line of which Mergal had spoken. A whisper as faint as thought spurred him to run back toward Township.

The whisper expanded to a hiss, a snarl, and then a distant rumble. Tharo glanced over his shoulder. The skyline frothed like a rabid beast as Bawror continued to climb into the sky, exposing the black scars at its base.

The princess cried, jolted by Tharo's strides as he pounded across the sand. No time to soothe her. If he didn't reach Township before the sea...

The rock climbed above the horizon, but the rumble of the oncoming deluge grew too. It became deafening, drowning out Drinith's wails. Tharo kept his gaze fixed on Township. As long as he didn't glimpse the wall of water sweeping toward them, he could pretend he might yet outrun it.

On the summit of Township, Mergal waved. The sea swallowed his shout, but he pointed to the new net dangling down the rock. Tharo grabbed it and started to climb. Drinith, in her sling, forced him to lean back as he scrambled up the wobbling, shifting ladder.

Tharo cradled her with one arm as Mergal heaved him over the ledge. "Mind the baby!" But even he couldn't hear his yell. Mergal pulled him into a hut and slammed the door shut. The approaching water's roar followed them into the pitch darkness. Tharo held Drinith close and tried to calm her. The ground shook as, outside, the sea slapped the rock's prow. The thunderous roll gradually subsided.

Eventually the door creaked open and Mergal scanned outside.

"Where are you going?" Tharo demanded.

"Come and take a look," Mergal said. "You can leave your baby here."

Easy for him to say. Tharo comforted Drinith until she calmed. He placed her on a grubby mat and followed Mergal outside.

Frothing waters stretched from horizon to horizon.

"The sea follows Bawror," Mergal said. "It will leave again and the desert will return." He gazed up at the three moons. "My people will be here soon with supplies. You can get passage on my sons' ship to the port of Skander."

Hopefully this flood has caught the souldiviners and drowned them. As if summoned by the thought, the familiar tingle returned. As it expanded, Tharo stared into the angry, spitting water surging past. *That's right. That's coming for you, you monsters.* The buzz came to an abrupt stop. Tharo laughed until Mergal's quizzical gaze sobered him.

Mergal beckoned him back inside the little hut. "Come and have some dried fish."

Drinith's lament wafted through the doorway. Tharo's sigh ended in a smirk. She never gave him a moment's rest. He picked her up and gently coddled her. "What's wrong now? Wet? Hungry? Tired?"

She yawned.

"Ah, tired," Tharo said, placing her dummy in her mouth. He sang a lullaby, the only one he could remember, the one his mother sang to him. Her eyelids slowly fluttered shut. Her ability to fall asleep to his gravelly, tuneless rendition remained the highest compliment his voice had ever received.

Tharo kissed her on the cheek and laid her down. "Dream well, little one." As he glanced around the room, the horror in Mergal's stare held him. "Are you all right?"

"Yes." The quiver in Mergal's voice suggested otherwise. He walked over to the door and gazed at the sea. Had he recognized the gem on her forehead? The Kaplar Empire must be known even in this distant land. Had Mergal realized who Drinith was and who might be after her?

———

The following days passed like a pleasant dream for Tharo. Despite Mergal's promises to the contrary, the stormy sea girdling their humble refuge appeared to be as permanent and unyielding as the desert it replaced. Staring at this vast expanse of water bounded only by the sky, it was easy for Tharo to imagine the whole world drowned, and with it any threat to his charge.

The cessation of the souldiviners' attacks encouraged this fantasy. The flood must have taken them. Hopefully the phial of his blood had drowned with them. Of course, it wasn't over. Another group of souldiviners would be dispatched to hunt him. Even without his blood, they would find him eventually. But for now, at least, he could pretend his trial had come to an end.

Mergal's peculiar wariness around him mellowed, and they became friends. Mergal proved to be amicable company. When cooped up in their little cabin by the sporadic torrential rains that accompanied the sea, they swapped stories. Tharo poorly recounted Kaplar sagas and the adventures of other Warserks. Aside from the unseemliness of mentioning his own exploits, his failure to save his emperor soured them. Tharo enjoyed Mergal's stories of the desert and the sea, so different from the folktales of the highlands and yet sharing a common humanity. And Tharo appreciated his host's scrupulous avoidance of questions about Drinith.

When the red sails of the returning flotilla finally prodded above the wind-tossed horizon, it felt like an intrusion on his peace.

Mergal smiled by his side, his arms folded. "Get ready to leave. As soon as my sons' boat docks, I'll talk to the captain, my eldest, Ibroen. You, climb on board." His eyebrows knitted together. "There's a cabin where you can keep your daughter hidden. My sons don't need to know about her. Your daughter is your own business. Nobody else's."

If only Drinith was Tharo's daughter. If only he could watch her grow up here in untroubled anonymity. "Thank you," Tharo said, offering his hand.

Mergal threw his arms around him. "Look after yourself. And thank you for your stories. The word is worth more here than any riches."

Tharo patted him on the back.

By the time the boat drew alongside the rock, he stood ready to climb aboard. Beneath his cloak, Drinith slumbered in her sling, oblivious to the journey ahead.

One of the five crewmen threw a rope to Mergal. Another, a young boy, leapt onto the rock and helped pull the boat against it. Leather bags along its side cushioned it against the black stone. Mergal nodded to Tharo. "Hop on."

As he stepped across the narrow gap onto the boat, the oldest looking of the crew turned to Mergal. "Who's this highlander?" This one must be Ibroen.

"You're taking my good friend, Tharo, to the port of Skander," Mergal said. He turned to the son standing by his side and pointed to the boat. "Skillen, get back on board."

"But Father, what about the Homecoming Festival?" another youth protested.

"There's no time for celebrating when there's work to be done," Mergal said. "You're all young. You have many more festivals ahead of you."

Tharo ignored the disgruntled glances of his new companions.

"It'll be a long trip sailing against the current," Skillen whined as he stepped back on board.

Ibroen shielded his eyes as he looked up at the flag atop the mast. "At least the wind is with us, what there is of it."

Mergal loosed the two ropes and winked at him. "And when you return, I have wonderful stories to tell you! Wonderful stories!"

———

A painful drone in Tharo's head woke him. He closed his eyes, covered his ears, and held his breath. The souldiviners mustn't see where he was. They mustn't catch the scent of saltwater, or hear the creak and groan of the ship as it bounced on the waves. The pain burrowed through his brain like some flesh-eating grub.

The door of the cabin swung open. "Are you all right?" Ibroen asked him.

"Black sails!" someone cried outside.

The pain ceased. *No! No!* The souldiviners must be on the approaching ship.

"You fools!" Tharo roared as he crawled to his feet. Pushing past Iboren, he staggered out the door and gazed in horror upon the approaching vessel, a seagoing fortress flying Javlohm's flag—the Tree of Bones. As it furled its sails, arcs of spray rose in front of its bow.

"It's a Javlohm warship," Ibroen growled. "Is it hunting you?"

Tharo bowed his head. "Yes."

"I'll do my best to outrun it, but it's drawn by armored fish and we've nothing but sail."

If Warserks crewed this boat, Tharo wouldn't think twice about sacrificing every one of them to protect Drinith, but the lives of Mergal's sons weren't his to throw away in some valiant but hopeless gesture. "Steer toward it and invite the Javlohmers on board. Give them no reason to sink your vessel."

"What about you?" Ibroen asked.

What about Tharo? He stared into the rolling sea. The honorable course would be to drown himself and Drinith, but he couldn't bring himself to hurt her though it might spare her worse suffering. As long as she remained hidden in a corner of the cabin, a slim chance remained that she might be missed in any search. The crew's ignorance of her presence on board might yet save her. The souldiviners, so certain of their infallibility, might not even bother searching the ship after probing their minds. As long as Tharo didn't live to betray her.

"I'll be back momentarily," he said, dashing into the cabin. He removed the cloth over the modest box containing Drinith. She looked so peaceful, asleep in her makeshift cot. His eyes burned as he gave her cheek a final kiss. With luck, by the time she awoke, the souldiviners would be gone. Then her cry would alert Mergal's sons of her presence. He covered her cot again and wrapped his cloak so to give the impression of a swaddled baby. He strode out onto the deck.

"What are you going to do?" Ibroen asked breathlessly.

Tharo kept glancing downward until the lowlander's wide-eyed stare turned to the cloth bundle cradled in his arms.

"What's that?" Ibroen asked.

"Something too precious to fall into the Javlohmers' hands." Tharo seized the gunwale with one hand and inhaled to steady his nerves.

"No!"

As Tharo lifted his leg, Ibroen grasped his shoulders and attempted to pull him away. Tharo bent his raised leg as he turned, driving his knee into Ibroen's side. Dazed, the young man released him, staggered backward, and toppled over.

As Ibroen's brothers helped him up, the souldiviners' buzz invaded Tharo's skull. Its bewildering pain slapped him to the deck. Never before had he suffered such agony.

Ibroen approached warily and picked up the dropped ball of cloth. His face clouded with puzzlement as it unfurled in his hands. Spray rained down on the ship, casting rainbows over the deck before the hulking shadow of the Javlohm vessel snuffed them out.

The drone ceased. "Whatever happens to me, stay out of this," Tharo croaked. Ibroen and the others had already begun to back away. Tharo tried to rise, but his arms couldn't take the strain. The attack had left him weak, hollow.

Skillen gave a curt gasp. Horror stretched his childish face as he stared down at the black bolt sticking out of his chest.

"No!" Tharo roared.

As the sons of Mergal reached for their toppling brother, Ibroen's hand shredded. They danced briefly to the rain of bolts before dropping. The volley continued, pinning their corpses to deck.

The metallic scent of blood overwhelmed the salty sea air. Tharo banged his fist against the floor. These men's only crime was helping a stranger. Was there no end to the Javlohmers' depravity? He banged his fist again and again, his anger rising with each rhythmic strike. He drew his dagger. This time it would taste someone else's blood. He might not be able to defeat the souldiviners and their minions, but they'd pay a heavy price for their victory. Yes, they would learn what a Warserk could do in battle.

Two figures in shimmering armor slid down ropes onto the deck—the souldiviners' henchmen, gauntlars. He bounded toward them. As they drew their swords, he drove his knife through the slit of the nearer gauntlar's visor. As it reeled backward, Tharo simultaneously seized the handle of its sword, swept it free of its scabbard, and drove it at the second gauntlar's helm. The gauntlar swung its head clear of the thrust. Its sword squealed against Tharo's breastplate as he slammed into the unstable monster, shunting it backward. It stumbled against the bulwark and flipping over the side, disappeared into the sea with a splash.

Retrieving his dagger from the other gauntlar's corpse, Tharo smirked. Let more come. He'd kill them too. He'd—

The souldiviners' drone pummeled him to the deck. The dagger and sword fell from his trembling hands.

A half-dozen more gauntlars descended. Three, no, four men in samite followed. Their empty oracular cavities stared down at Tharo. In the center of each of their foreheads were the organs that gave them their power—a glistening compound eye between a pair of translucent wings.

Two gauntlars seized Tharo and lashed him to the mast. As the souldiviners' wings closed over their eyes, his pain dissipated.

"So, here is the last Warserk," said the souldiviner with the smuggest grin. He rolled a glass phial in his fingers, lifting it up so that Tharo could see his blood within it. "You gave us quite a run. I feel I have you at a disadvantage since I know you very well, Tharo, and you have no clue who I am." He gave an appreciative nod toward his chuckling colleagues. "Permit me the pleasure of introducing myself." He pressed a hand to his chest. "My name is Scaphal. I am the Souldiviner General to His Imperial and Immortal Majesty Magian the Infinite of Javalohm."

Tharo bowed his head in defeat as Drinith's plaintive cries drifted through the open doorway of the cabin. Why did the Javlohmers ignore her? They probably wanted to linger over his humiliation first.

Scaphal approached him. How could he see where he went? Perhaps the tiny slit separating the folded wings over his eye provided him enough vision. "We owe you thanks. Your warning about the flood saved us."

Tharo groaned.

"We razed Godsdoor to find you, you know?" Scaphal's grin stretched. "The Oracle burned in his temple."

So, the Oracle had been right after all. How many times had Tharo cursed the poor man in the wrong?

Scaphal turned to his colleagues. "Gebbit, the princess." He lingered over each word.

A souldiviner glided into the cabin.

"Leave her alone!" Tharo raged. He burst into tears. "Leave her alone." But none of the Javlohmers listened, their attention fixed on the cabin. He glanced at the gauntlar beside him. The reflection of his tattoos on its armor, *honor* and *truth,* mocked him. He strained against bonds too stout to break. He had failed himself, his emperor, his people, and most of all, Drinith. She deserved better than to die at the callous hands of these murderers. "Let me die with her." Tharo choked on the words.

Scaphal sneered at him. "So, the last Warserk faces death weeping like a child."

Drinith's screams soared. Part of Tharo wanted more than anything not to see what horror emerged from the cabin. That part of him was a coward. But he must watch. He must bear witness to her death for the brief time before the souldiviners slew him.

The cabin fell silent. Tharo's anguished cry couldn't fill the silence.

Gebbit glided out of the cabin, clutching Drinith by the leg like a doll. The souldiviners turned to Tharo, their wings spreading. Their buzz filled his mind and expanded through his body. Every nerve stretched on the rack of its insistent probing. Let them kill him. It no longer mattered. Drinith was dead, dead, dead.

The buzz ceased. Scaphal lifted Tharo's bowed head by his hair. The grin had disappeared. "Where is the princess?"

Dumbfounded, Tharo stared at the doll Gebbit held. The Oracle's spell broke. The bittersweet emotions stirred by Tharo's sudden recollection of handing Drinith over to him expanded into a giddy elation. She still lived! She still lived! He grinned. "The Oracle left Godsdoor long before you reached it."

Scaphal's jaw wavered.

"We knew you would follow me there," Tharo said, his voice soaring with triumph. "And we knew you would keep following me as long as I believed I had the princess."

"The magic bottle was another toy," Gebbit said, tossing it with disgust on the deck.

"But we always catch our quarry," another souldiviner said with delicious dismay. Stripped of their daunting infallibility, the souldiviners looked so frail.

"Not this time!" Tharo thundered. Tears again welled in his eyes—tears of joy. "This time you've failed. By now, the princess is beyond your reach." And someday, Drinith would reclaim her crown.

Scaphal's shock turned to rage. "You won't live to tell anyone."

As the souldiviner drew his knife, Tharo's triumphant guffaw scorned him. The fortune-teller had been right after all.

A WORD FROM THE AUTHOR

Want to find out what happens next to Drinith? Continue the story with the novel **Fatal Shadow,** the first book in the **Champions of Fate** series.

The best way to learn about future releases in this series and my other works is to join my email list at https://photocosm.org/.

It would mean so much to me if you could leave an honest review wherever you purchased this story.

Feel free to email me at noelcoughlan@photocosm.org to ask any questions or share any comments you have about this book. I love to hear from readers.

Best wishes,

Noel

facebook.com/photocosm

twitter.com/noel_coughlan

goodreads.com/noel_coughlan

amazon.com/author/noelcoughlan

bookbub.com/authors/noel-coughlan

FATAL SHADOW

Long ago, magic cracked apart the world and suspended great continents between two suns. But the ebb and flow of human history continues. Trade and war cross the void on dragon wings. Great empires rise and topple...

As the rightful heir to one such fallen state, Drinith has known only exile, dashed hope, and constant threat. She has so far eluded the murderous intentions of the tyrant Magian the Infinite thanks to the prophetic visions of the oracle, Quiescat, but his power is failing. All he can glimpse in the future now is his own death.

An assassin's blade forces her into a desperate gamble. She takes her one final chance to secure the ally she so desperately needs. But at the end of her journey, she'll find deceit, betrayal, and murder. And she'll learn Magian isn't the only threat to her people.

Fatal Shadow is the first of six books in the **Champions of Fate** epic fantasy series. If you enjoy fast-paced action, intriguing characters, and imaginative world-building, then you'll love this engrossing novel.

THE GOLDEN RULE

Elf. Warrior. Saint. Heretic. Monster. Despised by two peoples, this pariah might yet prove to be the savior of both.

AscendantSun serves a dead god no longer. Adopting the religion of his human enemies, he haunts their mountains hoping to make amends for his violence toward them. Now, a figure from his past threatens to restart the ancient conflict he has struggled so long to put behind him.

War is coming again to the mountains, but this time he'll fight the legionaries he once commanded. Prophecy is against him. Numbers, too. But the greatest peril is the distrust of his human allies. Can he forge an effective alliance before the bright power rising in the east destroys them?

A Bright Power Rising and *The Unconquered Sun* compose **The Golden Rule**, a two-part epic fantasy for readers who enjoy unique and intriguing world-building.

SHORT STORIES

Fantasy:

The Fate Healer

Draston's master, Hamvok the Merciful, craves a royal ancestor or two to legitimize his tyranny. But every avenue of Draston's research has come to a dead end. To save himself from the tyrant's violent displeasure, he commits himself to a path of forgery and sacrilege, risking the wrath of not only the gods, but a far more terrible entity, the dreaded Fate Healer.

The Parting Gift

Certamen's god is dead. His people, the Ors, are broken and enslaved. He finds consolation in the knowledge that they are safe... But not for much longer. Their masters, facing decimation by disease, are growing desperate. Desperate enough to kill.

(Prequel to *A Bright Power Rising*.)

––––––––

Science Fiction:

Alienity

Four short stories about aliens ranging from humorous to deadly somber.

––––––––

Horror:

The Murder Seat

Dr. Herbert Marriott has a problem that only murder can solve. Luckily for him, the perfect weapon is locked away in his rundown museum, one too incredible for any court to accept. The cursed chair kills all who rest upon it. But will Herbert's victim be so easily drawn to her fate?

———

ACKNOWLEDGMENTS

I want to thank Pamela Guerrieri-Cangioli from Proofed To Perfection for copy editing and proofreading the story, and Nick Lloyd for beta reading it. Ivan Cakic created a fantastic cover, but I also want to thank the other designers who submitted designs. They were all of such high standard. A very special thanks to Mags Murphy, Louise Fitzsimmons, Alison Donovan, Michael Wheeler, John T.M. Herres, Vanessa Coughlan, Deirdre O'Gorman, Carmel Lynam, and everyone else who took part in the poll to pick the winner.

ABOUT NOEL COUGHLAN

Noel lives with his wife and daughter in the West of Ireland. He writes epic fantasy, science fiction and horror.

From a young age, he was always writing a book. Generally, the first page over and over. Sometimes, he even reached the second page before he had shredded an entire copybook. And you couldn't even recycle all that wasted paper back then.

When he finally wrote and published a book, it took him fourteen years. *The Golden Rule* became two books so let us be generous and say he averaged seven years per novel. He has gotten a little faster since then. Honest.

His hobbies include writing, reading, and reading about writing. He has written about reading in the past, and he still writes about writing. He would happily stay at home all day writing, but the family dog, Ruby, insists on taking him for daily walks.

His pet hates include writing his biography and referring to himself in the third person.